SUPERDOG IN TROUBLE

SUPERDOG IN TROUBLE

David Henry Wilson

Illustrated by Linda Birch

KNIGHT BOOKS
Hodder and Stoughton

A catalogue record for this title is available from the British Library

ISBN 0 340 58011 9

Printed and bound in Great Britain by
Cox & Wyman Ltd, Reading, Berkshire

Hodder and Stoughton Children's Books
A Division of Hodder Headline PLC
338 Euston Road
London NW1 3BH

Contents

The Amazing Me

Hello, Superdog-lovers. I thought I'd say a few woofs before telling you about my wonderful life. You all know who I am, of course – Woofer's the name, though you can just call me Superdog, as everyone else does.

I live with the Browns, or rather the

Browns live with me. Mr Brown is always nice but not very clever, Mrs Brown is sometimes nice and is far too clever, and Tony and Tina are my best friends, with Tina slightly bester than Tony. Tina is always nice and always clever. She reminds me of me.

Next door to us are the Thomases and their black and white tom-cat. Mr Thomas and the tom-cat are my great enemies, and I wish they'd move.

Three doors away from them are the Montagues, who live with Honey. Honey is the most beautiful she-dog in the world. I make no secret of the fact that I love Honey. Honey is a lot more secret than I am, but I think she loves me, too. She just doesn't show it.

When you're a superdog, life is full of excitement, and the three adventures in this book are *very* exciting. But in all three of them I was in trouble, and as I don't want you to get frightened, I'll tell you straight away that I got out of trouble again. A superdog always gets out of trouble. So don't worry. Just carry on reading and enjoying my thrilling adventures. I hope you'll finish up by admiring me as much as I do.

1
Lost

Lost! The very word strikes fear into the heart although, of course, being a superdog, I don't know the meaning of fear. Actually, being a superdog, I suppose I shouldn't have got lost in the first place, but when I tell you what happened, you'll see that it was quite understandable. I understand it, anyway. I'm pretty good at understanding things. Especially things that happen to *me*.

It was all a long time ago, when I was more a superpup than a superdog, and it began with the worst of all possible beginnings: a bath. There I was in my basket in the hall, having a quiet morning and doing no harm to anyone, when Mrs Brown uttered the dreaded words, 'It's time

Woofer had a bath.'

Anyone who knows me knows that it's never time I had a bath. I hate baths. Baths,

like cats and rubber bones and Mr Brown's slippers, ought to be abolished.

'Woofer! Here, boy!' called Mrs Brown.

Woofer stayed right where he was.

'Come on, Woofer! Bath time!'

I closed both eyes. I thought that if I closed my eyes, maybe she wouldn't see me. She saw me all right. One moment I was lying warm and relaxed and dry in my basket, and the next I was being whooshed up in the air, swooshed to the kitchen, and slooshed into a bathful of stinging soap and water.

'Stop wriggling!' snapped Mrs Brown.

'He doesn't like soap,' said Tina, who understands me almost as well as I do.

'And he doesn't like water,' said Tony, who understands me almost as well as Tina does.

'And *I* don't like smelly dogs,' said Mrs Brown, who understands dogs as little as she understands smells. Me, a smelly dog? My legpits smell as sweet as roast turkey in a rose garden.

I was really fed up with the soap, water, scrubbing-brush, and Mrs Brown. All the same, I shouldn't have done what I did. I understand why I did it, and I can even forgive myself for doing it because it was a

very understandable and forgivable thing to do, but I shouldn't have done it. I bit her.

I only bit her in the finger, and it wasn't a very deep bite. But I shouldn't have done it. I should have realised that she could hurt me a lot more than I could hurt her. Almost as fast as it takes to say 'Ouch!' she'd lifted

me out of the water, smacked my bottom, dried me, and put me outside the kitchen door.

'And there you'll stay,' she said, 'till you learn to behave yourself.'

Well, I certainly wasn't going to stay there *that* long. In fact, I wasn't going to stay there at all. I was furious. I stomped round the outside of the house, grumbling and growling. What a way to treat a dog! And a superdog at that! Who did she think she was? Who did she think *I* was? How dare she bath me, smack me, and put me out? *When I hadn't even had my breakfast!* It was too much. I let out a superhowl of bathed, smacked, put-out, breakfastless rage.

'Quiet, you horrible mongrel!' said a voice from next door.

I looked up and saw Mr Thomas glaring over the garden fence at me. Mr Thomas owns the black and white tom-cat and, as far as I'm concerned, he and the black and white tom-cat are like baths – they should be abolished.

'Grrrrr!' I said. Actually, I didn't say it, I just thought it. Mr Thomas isn't the sort of man you say 'Grrrrr!' to.

What a life! Now I couldn't even howl in

my own front garden. I'd had enough. If they didn't want me here, I'd go somewhere else. There would be plenty of people in the world who'd be only too pleased to look after a superdog without bathing him.

I squeezed through the bars of the garden gate, and set off to see the world. Just at that moment it started to rain. If I wasn't being wetted indoors, I was being wetted

outdoors. Everyone was determined to wet Woofer. I felt like giving up. But superdogs don't give up so easily. With the courage you've all come to know and admire, I trotted away through the rain, turning down one street and up another, round corners, through gardens, across roads. At least I was free now. Free to go where I pleased, as I

pleased, when I pleased. Free to run, walk, sit. Free to howl, yowl, growl. Free. And wet. And cold. And hungry.

I found myself in a field. It was a muddy field, full of cows quietly munching the grass. I don't think much of cows – silly fat bouncy things – but I was feeling a bit lonely, and talking to a cow is better than talking to nobody.

'Hello,' I said to the nearest one. 'You're

a nice fat bouncy cow.'

'Get lost,' she said.

'What was that?' I asked.

'Get lost,' she said again.

She was a very unfriendly cow, and I told her so. 'You're a very unfriendly cow,' I said.

'I'm not a cow,' she said, 'I'm a bull. And if you don't move out of this field right now, you'll get a nice fat bouncy horn just where

21

you don't want it.'

I didn't stay to find out where. I raced out of that field faster than a fly off a bull's back.

The next place I came to was a yard, and in the yard were chickens, clucking and strutting around as if they owned the place. At the far end I saw a sort of large box with a very yummy smell coming from it. It was a smell that filled my nose with thoughts of breakfast, but those chickens looked pretty fierce. Would I be able to get to the box?

Slowly, but very bravely, I took a few cautious steps forward. The chickens nearest to me squawked loudly and jumped out of the way. This was going to be easy after all.

'Get out of my way,' I said to the chickens that had got out of my way.

'Uck yuck cluck!' they squawked, falling over their own feet and feathers.

I stuck out my mighty chest, and

advanced towards the box. There were still a few birds pecking away at my breakfast, and so I growled a terrifying 'Grrrrrout of there!' which scattered them in a panic. Those chickens really were chicken. Just one silly creature had stayed behind. She had her back to me and her bottom in the air as she pecked away, obviously unaware of my superpresence. Maybe she was deaf. I decided to have a bit of fun. I crept up behind her, and then let out an egg-splitting 'WUFF!' which would have frightened any ordinary chicken out of her feathers.

But this was no ordinary chicken. She turned round and before I knew what was happening, she'd spread her wings, rushed straight at me, and pecked me right on the nose. I have a very sensitive nose, and it wasn't designed to be on the sharp end of a chicken's beak. Tears came to my eyes, and I had a sudden feeling that breakfast was a long way away.

'Hold on,' I said, 'there's no need for violence . . .'

But this chicken was fighting mad. There was a look in her eyes that spelt trouble with a capital peck, and the trouble was hitting me in the neck, the shoulder, the ribs . . .

'Stop it!' I said. 'That hurts!'

She didn't seem to care that she was hurting me. Some animals are really inconsiderate. Now I'm the bravest dog you'll ever meet, but this chicken had a beak, and I didn't, so it wasn't a fair fight.

On the other hand, I had four legs, and she only had two, so I used my legs. I used them to run out of that yard faster than a pea from a catapult.

Some way behind me I heard a very strange noise. It sounded like 'Cock-a-doodle-doo!' She certainly was no ordinary chicken.

Before I'd entered that yard, I'd been wet, cold and hungry. Now I was wet, cold, hungry, and pecked all over. Being free was no fun at all. The Browns would be sitting down for lunch now. Maybe a leg of lamb, cooked to perfection by Mrs Brown. They'd be cutting slices off a big, juicy bone. A bone that was meant for Woofer.

'Where's Woofer?' Tina would be asking.

'What's happened to Woofer?' Tony would ask.

'Anyone seen Woofer?' Mr Brown would ask.

'I wish I hadn't bathed him and smacked

him and put him outside,' Mrs Brown would say. At least, I think she'd say that.

And where *was* Woofer? Even poor old Woofer didn't know. He was wandering lost and miserable along a country road, Tinaless, Tonyless, leg-of-lambless . . .

Most dogs would have given up. They'd have sat down, sighed, cried, and died. That's what I felt like doing, anyway. I did sit down, in fact. And I did sigh, and I did have a little cry, but I definitely didn't die. If I'd died, I wouldn't have been able to tell you this story, would I? No, superdogs are not like most dogs. And this special superdog took a decision that needed special superdog intelligence to take. I decided to go home.

Perhaps you're surprised. Well, I'm not. I'd do the same even now. Though I wouldn't need to make a decision like that now. You won't catch me running away again. Once pecked, twice shy.

There was just one problem. How was I going to find the way? Fortunately, my supersensitive nose hadn't been too badly damaged, and so I didn't have much trouble picking up my own sweet, turkey-rose scent. It had stopped raining, too, which made it easier to follow the trail. But when your nose is to the ground, it's impossible to have your eyes up in the air, and the next thing I knew was that I was staring at the long, curved toenails of:

'Cock-a-doodle-doo!'

I was back in the yard with the chickens! I wasn't there for long, I can tell you. Before

you could split a doodle from a doo, I'd gone again. I moved so fast I thought for a moment I'd left my back legs behind. I hadn't, of course. They were following my front ones.

Now what was I to do? There was no point in sniffing my own trail any more. If I did, I'd end up on the horns of the bull. I couldn't go forward, I couldn't go back, I couldn't go anywhere. And so I did what most dogs would have done: I gave up. I sat down, sighed, cried, and got ready to die.

It was a clever move. I'd hardly laid my sore nose down on the wet grass when I heard a voice.

''Allo, dog,' it said.

I raised my head, and saw a very dirty man with a torn raincoat, a stubbly beard, and a battered suitcase.

'Yer lookin' a bit sorry fer yerself,' he said.

I let out a sorry-for-myself whine.

'Lost, are yer?' he said.

I let out a sorry-for-myself, lost whine.

'Lost an' 'ungry, from the look of yer.'

I let out a sorry-for-myself, lost-and-hungry whine.

'Well, let's 'ave somethin' ter eat,' he said.

They were the first cheerful words I'd heard all day.

From his bag he pulled out a packet and, when he took the paper off the packet, I smelt a smell that came straight from heaven. Beef. That's what it was. A thick sandwich of juicy, meaty, made-for-Woofer beef. The smell pulled me to my feet as if

my nose was on the end of a lead.

'Smells good, don' it?' said the man.

Good? It was the Smell of the Century. The smell-waves had gone up my nostrils and down into my jaws, and my tongue was almost falling out with excitement. Oh beef, beef, come to Woofer . . .

''Old on,' said the man. 'It ain't all fer

you. Yer'll 'ave ter share it wiv me. 'Alf an'
'alf, okay?'

He broke the sandwich in two, and
reached down to give me my half. Oh, that
beef sandwich, or rather half sandwich . . .
without doubt it was the beefiest, sandiest
wichiest piece of yum-yum I had ever
scrunched in my life. I could have eaten it

all over again. Ten times.

'That's the lot, doggy,' he said. 'It's all gorn.'

It hadn't. There was still a little chunk in his hand. I could see it. I could see nothing else. The whole world had shrunk to a little chunk of beef sandwich. If only . . .

'Orl right,' he said. 'You c'n 'ave it.'

I had it. And then it was all gone.

'Now then,' said the man, 'let's see where yer live, eh?'

I let him look at my collar.

'Woofer, is it? Hm, we'd better get you 'ome, Woofer, 'cos yer fam'ly might be worried about yer.'

He felt in his bag again, and for one glorious moment I thought he might be about to produce another beef miracle, but instead he pulled out a long piece of string. This he tied round my collar, and then the two of us walked together back along the

road. We came to the cow-field, and stopped to look inside.

'Some prime beef in there,' said the man.

The unfriendly bull was standing quite near, and took a step towards me.

'You again,' he said. 'I thought I told you

to get lost.'

'You mind how you talk to me,' I said, 'or I'll have you in a sandwich.'

I was pretty tough even in those days. It was lucky for that bull that there was a gate and a fence between us.

The man and I walked on, across roads, past gardens, round corners, down one street, up another, occasionally stopping to ask the way, until at last I knew just where we were.

'Steady on, Woofer,' said the man, 'yer'll 'ave me arm off at this rate!'

And then we were walking through my very own garden gate. The man rang the front doorbell, the door opened, and . . .

'It's Woofer!' cried Mr Brown.

I nearly strangled myself leaping into the hall on one end of the string while the man held on to the other.

'Woofer!' cried Tony and Tina, bounding out to meet me.

'Hello, Woofer!' cried Mrs Brown, emerging from the living room.

'We thought we'd lost him,' said Mr Brown.

'Found 'im up near Laycock's Farm,' said the man. ''E was lyin' in the grass

there, whinin' an' pinin'. Give 'im 'alf me beef sandwich I did, 'cos he was lookin' so mis'rable.'

Well, it was almost worth being miserable just to enjoy being happy again. Tony and Tina made a great fuss of me, and Mr and

Mrs Brown made a fuss of the dirty man. Mrs Brown gave him a hot meat pie, and Mr Brown gave him a five-pound note.

'My lucky day, this is,' said the dirty man. 'I'm glad I met you, Woofer.'

Most people are glad to meet a superdog, but I was glad I'd met him, too. I'll always remember that beef sandwich.

When the dirty man had gone, the family all crowded round me to hug and pat me, and I resolved that I'd never run away from home again, whatever happened.

'Oh dear,' said Mrs Brown. 'Just look at the state he's in. Come on, Woofer, let's give you a nice warm bath.'

I let her do it. I didn't even bite her finger. Even if she hadn't learnt her lesson, I'd certainly learnt mine.

2
The Other Dog

Honey lives four doors away. It's one of my greatest achievements to be living in the same street as Honey. What beauty! What class! What yum-glug-cor-superness! When I go to Heaven, they'll only need to carry me four houses along the street.

A little while ago, I had a nasty experience. I was out for a walk with Mr Brown (I take him out every day, because he needs the exercise), and we met Mrs Montague. She was walking with Honey and, to my horror, another dog.

I always go a little weak at the knees when I see Honey. It's not that I'm shy – how could a superdog be shy? – but somehow I never know what to say to her. How do

Superdog in Trouble

you talk to perfection? And now the presence of this other dog made it even more difficult. I decided to take no notice of him. I just looked straight at Honey – or rather, I looked at the pavement just in front of Honey – and with great courage said something like 'Er . . . um . . .' Then I had a clever idea.

'Hello, Honey,' I said.

It was a good way to start a conversation.

She looked at me with those steak-and-kidney-brown eyes, and suddenly I found myself kneeling down, licking the pavement.

'Ugh!' she said.

It was a beautiful sound, and I knew it was meant just for me.

'Who's the mongrel?' asked the other dog.

I took an instant dislike to him. He was bigger than Honey. Good-looking, I suppose, in a nasty sort of way – glossy

coat, bushy tail, big brown eyes. He was rather like Honey, in fact, but I could tell straight away that he was not the kind of dog I'd want for a friend.

'It's Woofer,' said Honey. 'Though he calls himself Superdog.'

'Heughl, heughl, heughl,' sniggered the other dog. 'What's super about him?'

'What have you got to heughl about?' I snapped. 'I'd rather be super like me than

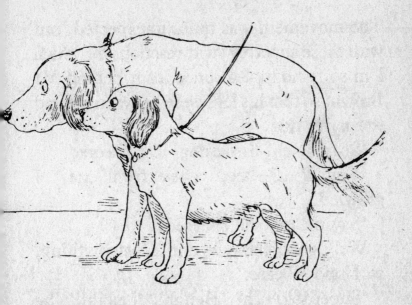

ugly like you.'

Although I say so myself, it was a smart reply. Honey probably hadn't realised how smart I could be. I was pretty surprised myself.

'Oh I say, I say, I say,' said the other dog, lifting his nose in the air as if he'd just smelt a cow-pat, 'the mongrel barks. Woofy, woofy!'

Then suddenly he jumped towards me.

The movement was quite unexpected, but with those superbly swift reactions for which I'm so famous, I at once leapt behind Mr Brown, so that his legs were between me and the nasty dog.

'Scared, eh, Superdog?' he sneered.

'You k . . . keep away from me,' I growled.

'Say please,' he sneered.

Well, good manners don't cost anything, so I said 'Please.'

'Superdog, eh? Heughl, heughl!' he sniggered.

He was obviously trying to make me look silly in front of Honey and, if I didn't do something quickly, he might succeed. On the other hand, he was a lot bigger than me. I decided to keep quiet for the moment. In any case, I couldn't think of anything to say.

'Come on, Woofer,' said Mr Brown at last.

'Come on, Honey. Come on, Simba,' said

The Other Dog

Mrs Montague.

'Goodbye, Honey,' I said.

'Ugh, ugh,' she replied.

I had a feeling that Simba might already have turned her against me. But I waited until we were some distance away, and then I let him have it:

'I shan't be so polite next time, Simba, you ugly pug! So there!'

That must have scared him. He didn't even dare to turn round. He let out a sort of heughl, heughl sound and just walked on, pretending he hadn't heard.

All the same, I didn't like the thought of my beautiful Honey walking with such a loud-mouthed, sniggering, pompous pedigree pooh. Friends like that can be a bad influence. If he kept telling her I was a mongrel and not a superdog, she might just possibly start to believe him. And how would that affect her feelings for me?

The more I thought about this Simba, the less I liked him. Honey had to be warned. And so the next day, after I'd had breakfast, I went straight to the front garden and stayed there all morning, keeping watch for her. Once I slipped out to have a sniff around her garden gate, but there was no scent of her anywhere. I left a little souvenir of myself on the gatepost.

When Mrs Brown called me for lunch, I was in trouble. Should I watch for Honey and miss lunch, or have lunch and maybe miss Honey? Lunch, I must confess, is an important part of my day. Together with breakfast and supper, it's really the *most* important part of my day. But could I risk leaving the garden?

Could I risk *not* leaving the garden? If I didn't have lunch, I'd starve. If I starved, I'd die. And if I died, I couldn't warn Honey. Therefore I had to have lunch.

'There you are, Woofer,' said Mrs Brown. 'I was beginning to think you'd got lost again. Come on, then.'

It was worth coming on for. Liver and

onions . . . mmmmm . . . I'd been quite right not to miss lunch. There aren't many greater pleasures in life than a dish of liver and onions. I treated them to my complete range of scrunching, humming, and slurping, then licked the dish, licked the floor round the dish, licked my lips, licked round my lips, and finally raced back into the front garden.

No sign of Honey. And the only smell on her gatepost was that of turkey-rose me. I was just lifting my leg to leave her a

refresher when suddenly I heard the sound of voices in the Montagues' back garden. Dog voices. Two dog voices. One was gentle and ear-sweetening and knee-weakening – the unmistakable sound-of-music melody of Honey. The other voice was Simba's.

I had to see her, and save her from this menace. But how? The side door was firmly closed. I'd have to go through the other back gardens. Home I raced, gasping with excitement and liver and onions.

The first garden I'd have to cross was Mr Thomas's. Now crossing Mr Thomas's garden would be about as safe as tiptoeing across a bull's horns. If Mr Thomas didn't get me, his black and white tom-cat would. Of course, being a superdog, I'm not afraid of anything, but if I was, Mr Thomas and his tom-cat would head the list of things I'd be afraid of. I thought of digging a tunnel, but that would have taken too long. And I thought of flying, but that would have taken even longer, since I didn't have any wings. And so, with the courage that I have come to admire so much, I poked my nose through the garden fence.

There was no Mr Thomas, and there was no tom-cat. My courage became even more admirable. I ran so fast across Mr Thomas's lawn that the grass must have thought I was a puff of wind.

Next-door-but-one was no problem, because an elderly couple lived there, and even if they saw me, they'd never be able to catch me. And next-door-but-two was no problem either, because the young couple who lived there were out at work all day. And next-door-but-three was Honey's house, and there she was, running round a tree being chased by Simba. How could she play such silly games? And with him? If she'd wanted to be chased round a tree, why hadn't she asked me to do it? I'd have

chased her round a tree all day if she'd asked me.

I stood between two gooseberry bushes and miserably watched them enjoying themselves. Then suddenly Honey spotted me. Those liver-brown, gravy-brown, dinner-brown eyes never missed anything.

'Ugh!' she said. 'Look what the wind blew in.'

Simba turned and looked.

'Ouf!' he said. 'It's Superstink.'

It was the perfect moment for one of those brilliant replies that spring so naturally to my lips, but this time nothing sprang so I kept quiet and just stood there. It was the right thing to do.

'What are you standing there for?' asked Honey.

Yes, indeed, she was actually speaking to me. And she was asking me a question. So she wanted me to speak to her. I'd come a long way in these few moments.

'I . . . um . . . I wanted to . . . er . . . talk to you,' I said.

'Oh I say, how exciting for you, Honey,' sneered Simba. 'A conversation with Superstink!'

'I'm not Superstink,' I said, 'I'm Superdog.'

'Heughl, heughl, heughl,' he sniggered. 'Not from where I'm standing!'

Even Honey sniggered. I knew he would be a bad influence on her.

'Please don't take any notice of him . . .' I said.

'Go away, Woofer,' she said. 'You're spoiling the air.'

It was a wonderful moment. It was the very first time she had called me by my name. Hearing her say 'Woofer' was like hearing Mrs Brown say 'lunch' ten times over. I think human beings call it 'poetry'.

'Did you hear what the lady said?' growled Simba. 'You're spoiling the air, so go away.'

'Thank you, Honey,' I said.

I wonder if she had the same feeling when I spoke *her* name. If she did, she kept her feelings to herself.

'Chase him off, Simba,' she said.

Maybe the emotion had been too much for her.

I was still listening to the twentieth echo of Honey's 'Woofer' in my ears when Simba bit me. He took me completely by surprise. Otherwise I'd have taught him a fighting lesson. But, as it happened, he bit me in the bottom, and I have a very sensitive bottom. And before I could do anything about it, the pain of that nip went from my bottom down into my legs, which carried me at top speed straight out of Honey's garden, across the

lawn of next-door-but-two, through the flowerbeds of next-door-but-one, and out on to the lawn of next door . . .

In the middle of Mr Thomas's lawn sat the black and white tom-cat. That was the moment at which the pain in my bottom suddenly stopped driving my legs.

'Yoiks!' I said, skidded to a halt, turned, and before the tom-cat could flap a whisker I was racing back through the flowerbeds of next-door-but-one, across the lawn of next-door-but-two, and . . . now where was I to go? One way Simba, the other way tom-cat. It was like being caught between a wild bull and a mad chicken.

The Other Dog

Most dogs would have panicked and run blindly into one trap or the other, but Woofer isn't like most dogs. My superbrain instinctively came up with the perfect solution. Simba to the right, tom-cat to the

left, so Woofer, master of tactics, stayed right in the middle. I didn't move. I sat down under an apple tree, and waited. And waited. And waited.

Night was beginning to fall when Mr Brown came for me. The Johnsons had come home from work and seen me under the apple tree. Mr Johnson had come out into the garden and tried to get me to move, but of course I stayed where I was because under the apple tree was the safest place to be, and so he'd gone to fetch Mr Brown. He probably thought I was ill. But I wasn't ill. I was clever. As soon as Mr Brown came, I rose to my feet, and the two of us walked home together. The tom-cat wouldn't have dared to attack me with Mr Brown at my side. And he wouldn't have dared to attack Mr Brown with me at Mr Brown's side. So we were both safe.

I never saw Simba again. And it was some time before I saw Honey, but when I did,

I was surprised how fat she'd got. I was so surprised that I mentioned it her – very tactfully, of course.

'You've got fat, Honey,' I said.

'I'm not fat, you stupid mongrel,' she said. 'I'm pregnant.'

My mother had told me all about pregnancy. She'd been pregnant just before I'd been born.

'Does that mean you're going to have puppies?' I asked.

My knowledge of these things was pretty impressive.

'Well, I'm hardly likely to have piglets,' she replied.

I must say I still haven't quite understood that remark.

Mr Brown said goodbye to Mrs Montague, and so I didn't have a chance to ask what had happened to Simba. The important thing, though, was that he'd gone, and my guess was that she'd got fed up with him. If she'd decided to have puppies, she certainly wouldn't have wanted him around when she became pregnant. Besides, Honey was far too intelligent to prefer a Simba to a superdog.

3
I Save the Family

It was cold. It was skin-pimpling, bone-cutting cold. It was so cold that my nose froze. That's how cold it was.

But the living room was warm because Mrs Brown had lit a log fire in the fireplace, and so we all sat in there and watched television. At first I hadn't even bothered to watch television. I'd gone straight up to the fire, sat down in front of it, and watched the flames instead.

'Come away from there, Woofer!' said Mrs Brown. 'You're completely blocking the fire.'

That was mean. I was enjoying myself in front of the fire, and I wasn't blocking it at all – it was blazing happily away, warming me all over. But if Mrs Brown tells you to come away, you come away. Or I do. So I sat by the radiator and watched television.

They were showing pictures of how cold it was. Snow and ice everywhere, rivers frozen, roads blocked . . . well, we didn't need the television to tell us how cold it was. You only needed to stick your nose out in the hall.

After the pictures of the cold, there was a film about people lost in the desert – blue sky, hot sun, golden sand. They didn't know how lucky they were.

After Tony and Tina had gone to bed, the grown-ups (Mr and Mrs Brown and I) went on sitting warmly in the living room until Mr Brown said something I didn't want to hear. 'Come on, Woofer, old boy,' he said. 'Time for beddies.'

Beddies meant the basket under the stairs. and the stairs were out in the hall. And the hall was out in the cold. I pressed up against the radiator and let out a pitiful whine that would have melted the ice round the coldest heart.

'Television's finished now, boy,' said Mr Brown. 'It's time for bed.' Mr Brown hasn't got a cold heart. Just a frozen brain.

'It's not the telly he wants,' said Mrs Brown. 'It's the radiator.' Mrs Brown hasn't got a frozen brain.

'Ah!' said Mr Brown. 'Shall we let him stay here?' Mr Brown has a warm heart.

'No,' said Mrs Brown, 'he might get into bad habits.' Mrs Brown has no heart at all.

Out I went, whining with misery, and completely wasting my whine. Then down I lay on my cold cushion in my cold basket, while Mr and Mrs Brown climbed the stairs, brushed their teeth, put out the light, and closed their bedroom door. Soon the house was totally quiet, except for the rattling noise in my mouth – that was my teeth. Oh, it *was* cold. There was icy air coming through the front door, and winding its way round the banisters, under the stairs, over my basket, and right into me. Cold? I'd have been warmer sitting in the fridge.

An ordinary dog would have curled up in his basket, gone to sleep, and woken up dead. Or rather, not woken up dead. But

a superdog is not an ordinary dog. You'll remember how my superbrain solved the problems of being lost in the country, and of being trapped between Simba and the tom-cat. Well, once again it came to my rescue with the cleverest of clever solutions. To stop freezing in the hall, I just had to get into the living room.

You might think that was difficult. You're probably wondering if I used my superstrength to break the door down, or bite a hole in it, or tunnel under the wall. I expect I would have done if I'd had to. But I didn't have to. One touch from my powerful paw was enough, and the door

opened. It knew who was boss. Or maybe
Mr Brown hadn't closed it properly.

I went in. Immediately I was covered in
a warm glow, and I marched triumphantly
towards the fire. But then I found that Mrs
Brown had put some sort of metal guard all
round it, which was really very selfish of
her. Not only did it stop the heat from
getting to me, but it also stopped me from
getting to the heat. Now what was I to do?

Well, the living room door hadn't stopped
me, and a metal guard wasn't going to stop
me either. The powerful paw that had
opened the door now forced its way between
guard and fireplace. One push and the guard
began its retreat. With paw and nose I
shifted it further still. And then with paw,
nose and shoulder I sent it staggering across
the hearth. Fortunately, it didn't fall –
otherwise it might have woken the Browns
up. A few more gentle pushes, and then
there was nothing between Woofer and a

warm night's sleep. If I could have twisted
my paw round far enough, I'd have given

myself a pat on the back.

I sat there for a while, enjoying the heat of the hearth on my bottom, and the glow of the fire on my face. The logs were still throwing out little flames, and occasionally making loud cracking sounds. I wondered if perhaps they might keep me awake, but they didn't. Once I lay down, I lay out.

The next thing I knew was pain. It was some way away from me, and yet it was part of me. A sharp, stinging pain. It woke me

up with a start. Where was I? Where was my basket? What was that smell? Ouch! What was happening to my tail? Ooh, aah . . .

I'll tell you what was happening to my tail. It was on fire. MY TAIL WAS ON FIRE! I leapt to my feet, and raced howling out of the room and up the stairs.

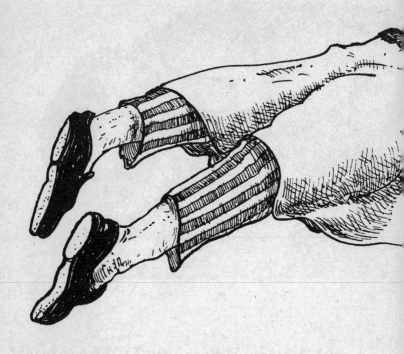

'Wowowowowowowowowowowowo!' I howled.

Out of his bedroom came Mr Brown, and I've never seen him move so fast. He hurled himself on to me, like me hurling myself on to a leg of lamb. I think he put out my tail-fire, but as he was lying right on top of me,

I couldn't see. I couldn't breathe either.

'If you're not careful,' said Mrs Brown, 'you'll crush him and suffocate him as well.'

'What's happened?' asked Tina's voice.

'What's wrong?' asked Tony's voice.

'Woofer's tail was on fire,' said Mrs

Brown. 'And Daddy's trying to save him by killing him.'

Mr Brown got off me, and I lay there wondering if I'd ever breathe, walk or wag again.

'How did his tail catch fire?' asked Tina.

'Good question,' said Mr Brown.

'He must have been in the living room!' said Mrs Brown.

'The living room!' cried Mr Brown, and

I Save the Family

I hadn't seen him move so fast since . . . well, since he put out my tail-fire. He raced downstairs like a man with a bull *and* a chicken after him, and the rest of the family followed. I followed, too, when I'd made sure I was still me.

When I got to the living room, Mr Brown was stamping on the carpet as if he was killing spiders, and Mrs Brown was thumping it with a cushion, as if she was knocking the spiders out. There was quite a lot of smoke in the room, and so Tony, Tina and I stayed in the doorway to watch.

'Phew!' said Mr Brown. 'I think we've done it.'

He and Mrs Brown looked down at the carpet, nodded, opened the window and came out into the hall, closing the door behind them.

'What happened, Daddy?' asked Tina.

'The living-room carpet was on fire,' said Mr Brown. 'Woofer came up to warn us.'

'Well done, Woofer!' cried Tony.

'Clever old Woofer!' cried Tina.

No one was more surprised than clever old Woofer, but I sat there quietly and modestly, letting them pat me and fuss over me.

'Woofer saved our lives, didn't he?' cried Tina.

'He's a hero!' cried Tony.

'He did,' said Mr Brown. 'And he is.'

And come to think of it, it was all true. If I hadn't gone racing up the stairs to wake them, the house could have been burnt down. I *had* saved them, and I *was* a hero. I began to feel pretty pleased with myself.

'Hm,' said Mrs Brown.

'What's the matter, dear?' asked Mr Brown.

'Well,' said Mrs Brown, 'I'm just wondering why the living-room door was open, how the guard got moved, and why Woofer's tail was on fire.'

Everyone stopped patting me and fussing over me. I suddenly went a bit cold, and my tail was sore, and I thought I might feel better if I lay down in my basket and had a rest. I began to creep towards the stairs.

'I've got a feeling,' said Mrs Brown, 'that Woofer didn't discover the fire at all. I think he started it.'

I'd almost reached my basket.

'Woofer, come here!' said Mrs Brown.

I came at once. I looked up at her lovingly, heroically, and you-can-trust-Wooferly.

'Now then,' she said, 'how did that tail of yours catch fire?'

I looked up at her adoringly, innocently, and un-fire-startingly.

'I know,' said Tina. 'He must have smelt the fire and gone into the living room to put it out. Didn't you, Woofer? That's why he moved the guard and got his tail burnt. Isn't it, Woofer?'

I love Tina. Tina sometimes reads my thoughts even better than I do.

'Whatever happened,' said Mr Brown, 'we would certainly have been killed if Woofer hadn't woken us up. So let's be thankful he did.'

And they all began to make a fuss of me again, which is how I like things to be. Then Mrs Brown made a hot drink for everybody, and I had a slice of roast turkey as a special reward. Mrs Brown also put some ointment

I Save the Family

on my tail, which stopped it stinging.

In the end, I slept quite well that night, snug in my basket under the stairs. It may have been cold outside, but being a hero made me feel nice and warm inside. In any case, superdogs don't feel the cold like ordinary dogs.

Another Knight Book

David Henry Wilson

SUPERDOG

'The greatest thing to hit the dog world since man invented biscuits.'

That's why he calls himself Superdog – though to the Brown family he's just plain old Woofer, and a bit of a nuisance, too. From falling into the lavatory to causing havoc in the supermarket, it's one disaster after another. But Tony and Tina Brown love him whatever he does, because children are very good at understanding dogs – even Superdogs.

The first book about the inimitable Superdog.

Another Knight Book

David Henry Wilson

SUPERDOG THE HERO

The Brown family call him Woofer, but he sees himself as Superdog. And when it comes to fighting daffodils, cricket balls and a runaway cow, he's certainly a superhero. Honey, the beautiful lady dog, and the black and white tom cat next door, might find it hard to believe it, but as Woofer himself says 'That's the great thing about us superdogs – nobody ever knows what we'll be up to next. Not even me.'

The second book about the inimitable Superdog.

MORE GREAT BOOKS AVAILABLE
FROM KNIGHT